To Elliana
& Nolan,

JaWt

In memory of Larry Gene Eaton, who showed me that dreams can be achieved.

www.mascotbooks.com

The Fantastic Voyage of Mr. Farfenoodle

For more information, please contact:
Mascot Books
620 Herndon Parkway, Suite 320
Herndon, VA 20170
info@mascotbooks.com

Library of Congress Control Number: 2018901094

CPSIA Code: PBANG0118A
ISBN-13: 978-1-68401-806-2

Printed in the United States

www.jaeaton.com

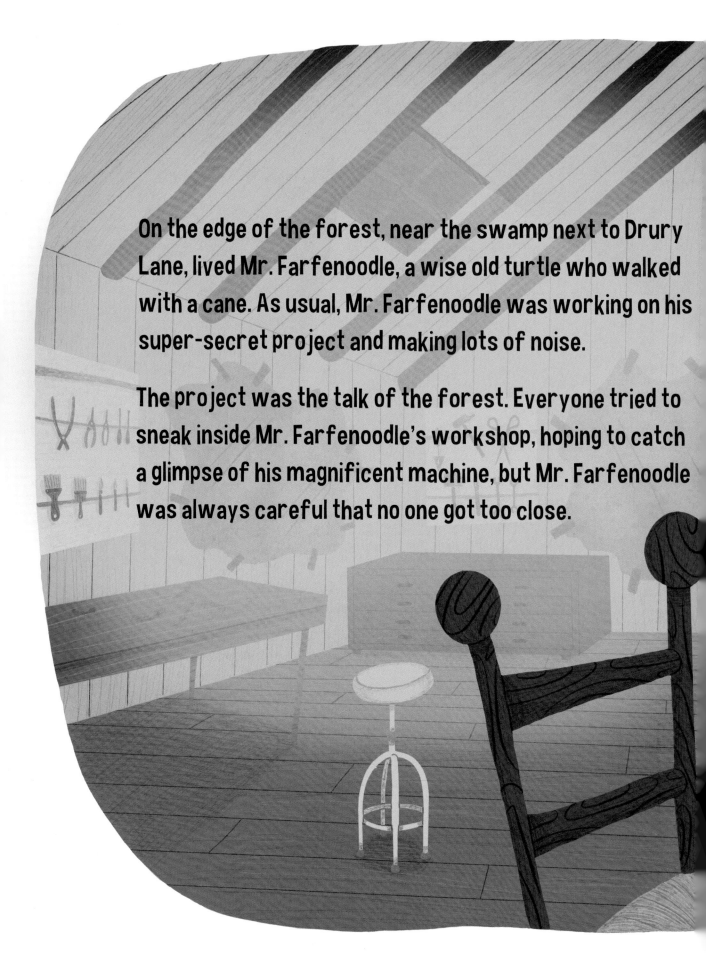

On the edge of the forest, near the swamp next to Drury Lane, lived Mr. Farfenoodle, a wise old turtle who walked with a cane. As usual, Mr. Farfenoodle was working on his super-secret project and making lots of noise.

The project was the talk of the forest. Everyone tried to sneak inside Mr. Farfenoodle's workshop, hoping to catch a glimpse of his magnificent machine, but Mr. Farfenoodle was always careful that no one got too close.

Codey the Cricket and Rudy the Raccoon sat outside Mr. Farfenoodle's house, wondering what their friend was up to. They could hear banging and clanging as he worked.

"I hope he's building an automatic ice cream maker!" said Rudy.

"You always talk about food!" laughed Codey.

"Well, us raccoons love food! What do you think it is?"

"Mr. Farfenoodle taught me to play the violin with my shorter leg, so he loves music. Maybe it's a machine that plays all the instruments of an orchestra at the same time!" exclaimed Codey.

Rudy laughed, and the friends spent the rest of the day coming up with ideas for Mr. Farfenoodle's secret project.

That night, Rudy quietly schemed and decided how he could get a peek into Mr. Farfenoodle's project. After his family went to bed, Rudy went back to the workshop. There was even more banging and clanging than earlier that day.

Rudy hid behind a bush until it went so quiet he could hear his stomach growl. When Mr. Farfenoodle finally turned off the lights and left, Rudy snuck inside.

Rudy couldn't believe his eyes when the moonlight shone on the secret project. It was a rocket ship!

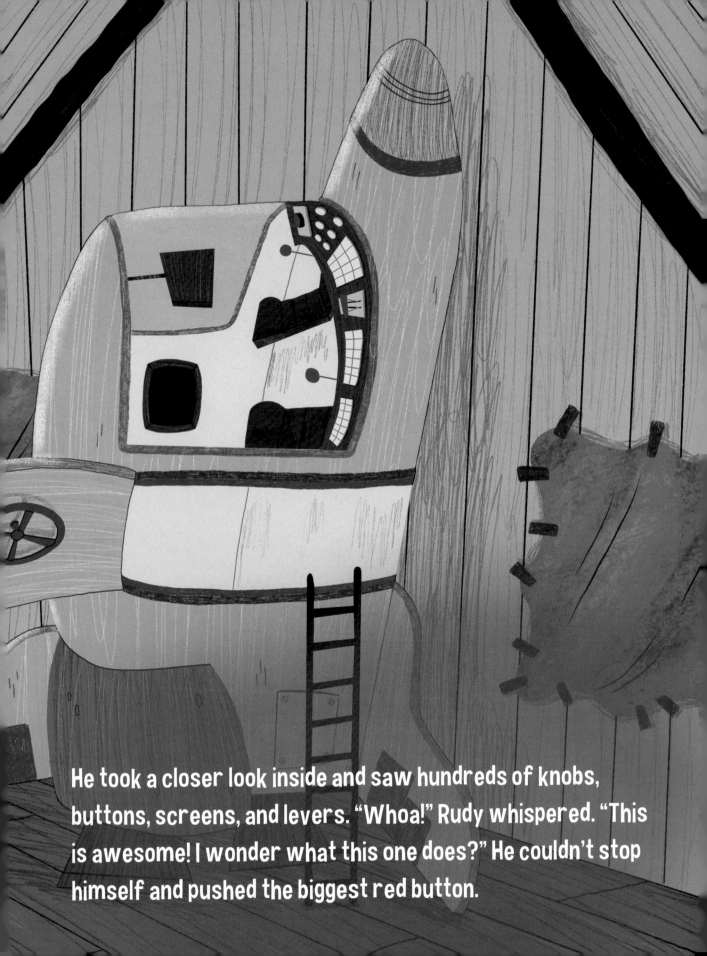

He took a closer look inside and saw hundreds of knobs, buttons, screens, and levers. "Whoa!" Rudy whispered. "This is awesome! I wonder what this one does?" He couldn't stop himself and pushed the biggest red button.

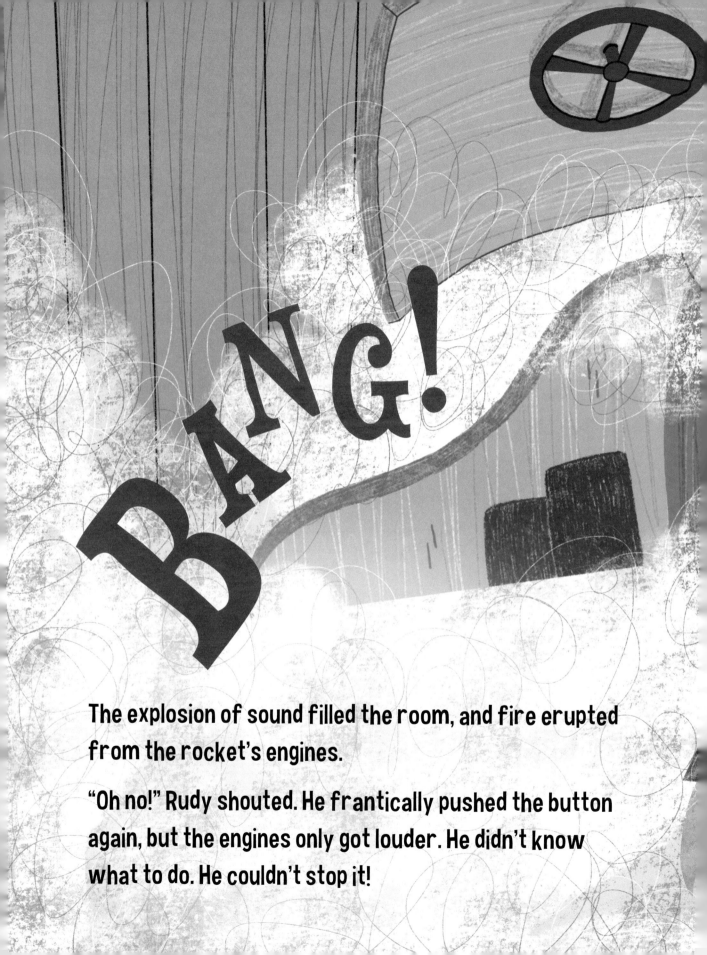

The explosion of sound filled the room, and fire erupted from the rocket's engines.

"Oh no!" Rudy shouted. He frantically pushed the button again, but the engines only got louder. He didn't know what to do. He couldn't stop it!

The hatch door swung open to a wide-eyed Mr. Farfenoodle. "Rudy!" he shouted. "What have you done?!"

"I'm sorry, Mr. Farfenoodle! I hit the big red button."

"Oh dear," Mr. Farfenoodle said. "Put your seat belt on. Once the liftoff button has been hit, I can't shut it down."

The computer began its countdown.

"Hang on!" Mr. Farfenoodle called. "We're about to launch!"

With an enormous whoosh, the rocket lifted off.

"Don't worry!" exclaimed Mr. Farfenoodle. "We'll be fine, but we're on our way to Pluto."

Rudy looked out the window and saw the moon. It was huge and getting closer by the second! "The moon looks like a gigantic sugar cookie."

"Oh, Rudy," Mr. Farfenoodle laughed, "how can you think about food at a time like this?"

The rocket picked up speed as it whizzed pass the moon. "We're headed to Mars next. Hold on tight. This may get a little bumpy."

The engines thrusted again as the rocket picked up speed.

"Whoa! Mars looks like a huge meatball."

The little rocket sped past Mars and approached an asteroid belt. Mr. Farfenoodle steered through the maze of humongous boulders.

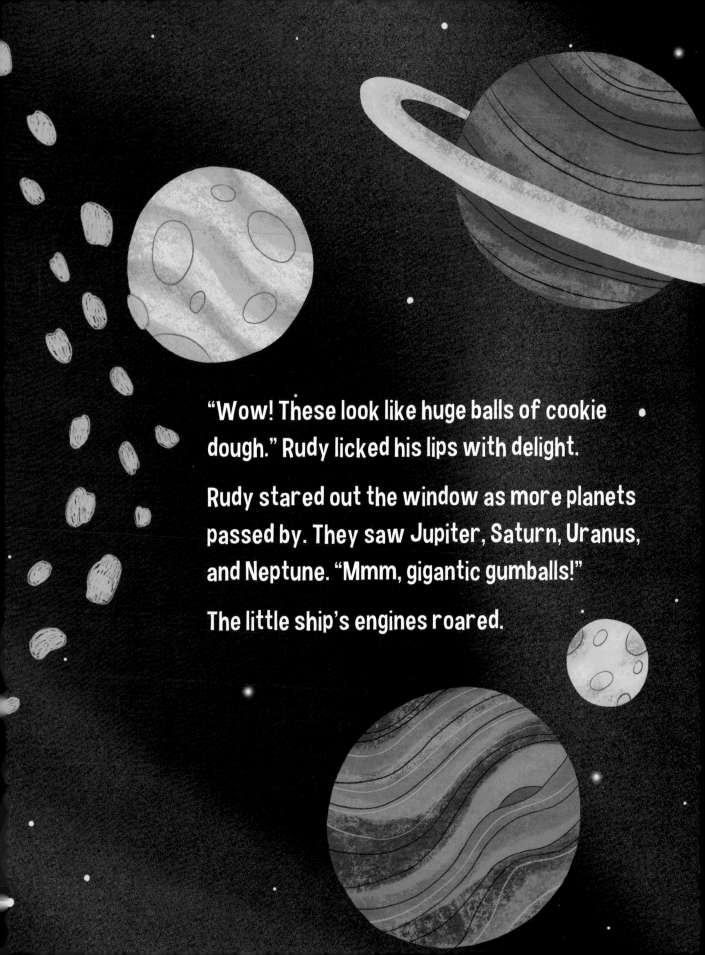

"Wow! These look like huge balls of cookie dough." Rudy licked his lips with delight.

Rudy stared out the window as more planets passed by. They saw Jupiter, Saturn, Uranus, and Neptune. "Mmm, gigantic gumballs!"

The little ship's engines roared.

When they finally reached Pluto, Mr. Farfenoodle
slowed the engines down. Rudy was amazed
they made it so far. Mr. Farfenoodle had
built a wonderful rocket ship!

"It's time to turn around. We must
get you and this ship back
home," said Mr. Farfenoodle.

The engines fired once again, making the
ship go even faster than before. The planets
were now passing by in reverse order and even
faster: Neptune, Uranus, Saturn, and Jupiter.

"Hold on tight, Rudy. Here comes the asteroid belt!"

"Yum! More cookie dough balls!"

Just then, Rudy saw in his window a little blue and green ball. "What's that?" he asked.

"That's Earth—our home," Mr. Farfenoodle answered.

"It's beautiful," Rudy said. "I can't wait until we're back. I'm starving."

After one final burst of the engines, the rocket ship began to slow down.

"I'm so sorry, Mr. Farfenoodle. I really made a mess of things," Rudy said.

"I forgive you," Mr. Farfenoodle said, "but let's keep your mistake our little secret!"

Rudy agreed, and together the two friends landed the rocket ship safely on the ground.

Rudy and Mr. Farfenoodle opened the hatch to cheers. All of their forest friends had come to see the rocket ship of Drury Lane.

"Hello everyone!" Mr. Farfenoodle called. "My assistant Rudy and I just made the most fantastic of voyages! Now that I know my rocket ship works, I'm excited to announce my new space shuttle service! You are welcome to book flights and join me for more fantastic voyages!"

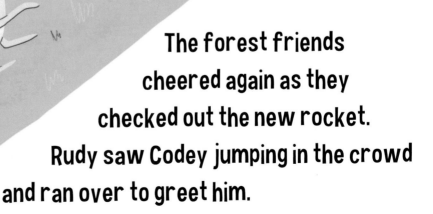

The forest friends cheered again as they checked out the new rocket. Rudy saw Codey jumping in the crowd and ran over to greet him.

"I can't believe you and Mr. Farfenoodle flew in a rocket ship. That's so cool!" Codey said.

"It was great," Rudy said. "All of the planets look like food."

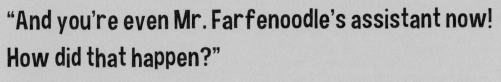

"And you're even Mr. Farfenoodle's assistant now!
How did that happen?"

Rudy laughed. "With the push of a big red button."

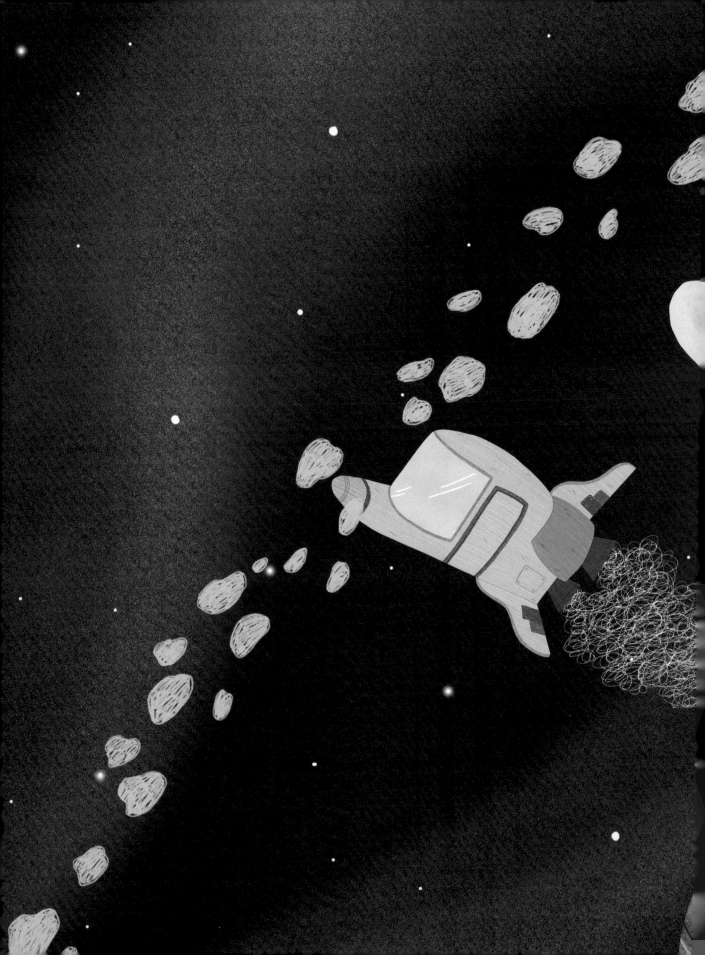